On the Day His Daddy Left

Eric J. Adams & Kathleen Adams, L.C.S.W.

ILLUSTRATED BY Layne Johnson

Albert Whitman & Company
Morton Grove, Illinois

To our boys. — E. J. A. and K. A.

Special thanks to Nathan, Angie, Luke, and Bridget. — L. J.

Library of Congress Cataloging-in-Publication Data

Adams, Eric J.

On the day his daddy left / by Eric J. Adams and Kathleen Adams;

illustrated by Layne Johnson.

p. cm.

Summary: On the day his father moves out of the house, Danny's teacher,

friends, and family reassure him that his parents' divorce is not his fault.

ISBN 0-8075-6072-3 (hardcover) ISBN 0-8075-6073-1 (paperback)

[1. Divorce—Fiction.] I. Adams, Kathleen (Kathleen Marion). II. Johnson, Layne, ill. III. Title.

PZ7.A21715 On 2000

[E]—dc21

00-008290

The design is by Scott Piehl.

On the day his daddy left, Danny woke up early, found his favorite purple marker, and in big letters wrote down a secret question. He folded the paper carefully and slipped it deep into the front pocket of his jeans.

On the day his daddy left, Danny didn't want to go to school, but his father promised he wouldn't leave until Danny got home.

Still, when Danny got to the playground, he didn't feel like playing. He leaned against the flagpole and touched his secret question.

"What's the matter?" asked his teacher, Mrs. Terry.

"Can you answer a question for me?"

"Of course," said Mrs. Terry.

Danny dug into his pocket, pulled out his secret question, and showed it to her.

She read the question and frowned. "Danny, where did you ever get such a silly idea?" she said. "Of course not. The answer is no. A BIG NO."

Danny felt better. Kind of. But not really.

When Danny got home on the day his daddy left, for a reason he couldn't explain, he just didn't feel like going inside.

Cindy was waiting with her brand-new bike. "Come on," she said. "Let's ride to the stop sign!"

Danny climbed on his bike, but he didn't ride very fast, not like usual.

"What *is* the matter with you?" Cindy asked.

"Your parents are divorced, right?" Danny asked.

"Yes," said Cindy.

"Can I ask you a question?"

"Shoot," said Cindy.

So Danny whispered the secret question in Cindy's ear.

Cindy sighed. "Sometimes I think it's true. You just can't worry about it, that's my advice. Come on, let's go to my house. My dad will fix us some lemonade."

But Danny didn't feel like going to Cindy's house for lemonade. Danny didn't feel like going anywhere on the day his daddy left.

On the day his daddy left, Danny watched his father pack his very last box. Then he sat on the curb next to Danny.

"I love you very much," said Danny's dad, "and so does your mother. Your life will be different, but it's going to be fine, I promise. I'll see you on Saturday, every Saturday, and we can do whatever you want. Okay?"

"Even rollerblading?" asked Danny.

"Even rollerblading," said his father.

Danny felt better. Kind of. But not really.

Danny's father hugged him, and Danny hugged him back. "Can I ask you a question, Dad?"

"Sure," said Danny's father.

Danny unfolded his secret question and watched his father read it.

"Oh, no. Please don't ever think this is true. *Never.* Promise?" said Danny's father.

Danny nodded yes, though he wasn't sure he could keep this promise as he waved his dad goodbye.

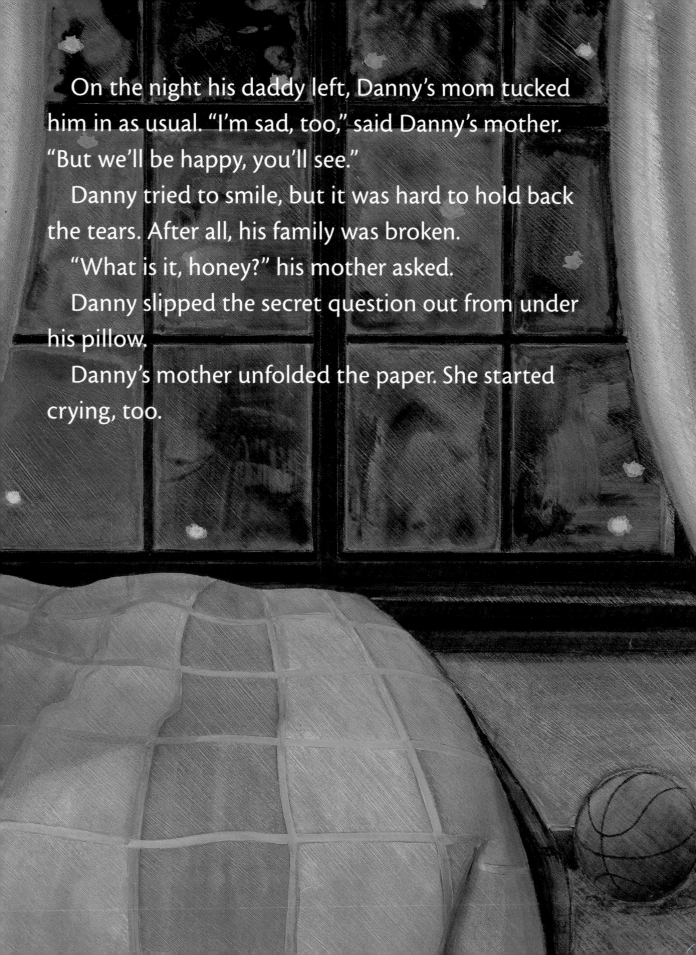

On the night his daddy left, Danny's mom tucked him in as usual. "I'm sad, too," said Danny's mother. "But we'll be happy, you'll see."

Danny tried to smile, but it was hard to hold back the tears. After all, his family was broken.

"What is it, honey?" his mother asked.

Danny slipped the secret question out from under his pillow.

Danny's mother unfolded the paper. She started crying, too.

"Well," Danny asked. "Is it true?"

Danny's mom hugged him tightly. "No, Danny, it's *not* true.

"It's not your fault. It's not your fault that your father is leaving. It's not your fault that we're getting a divorce. It never was your fault, and it never will be your fault. It's *our* fault, Danny, *our* fault, not yours."

Danny felt better. Kind of.

Danny's mother turned the paper over and with Danny's favorite purple marker she wrote a big NO on the back.

"Here," she said. "Keep your secret question with you always. Pull it out whenever you need to ask it. Then turn it over and look at the answer on the back. Because IT'S NOT YOUR FAULT."

And that's exactly what Danny did on the day after his daddy left.

And the days after,

and the days after that,

until his secret question fell apart from being unfolded
so many times.

Then one day, Danny's secret question flew away in the wind, but he kept on asking questions about the day his daddy left. Lots of questions.

And he always will.

Talking to Children about Divorce

Feeling guilty, like Danny's reaction in this story, is the most common reaction children have to divorce. But it's not the only one.

When parents divorce, children may experience intense feelings of worry, anger, grief, resentment, and hopelessness. They may doubt their parents' love or their own self-worth. They may even feel relief—and guilt over that relief—that the fighting will finally subside or that an abusive parent is leaving.

For the child, these emotions are a jumbled mess, and the inability to control the emotions causes yet more anxiety. It's up to the caring adult to help the child recognize and verbalize emotions and to realize that it's okay to feel all these things.

Listening is the greatest tool. When a child expresses an emotion, guide him or her to explore its causes. Explain that other children—and even adults—share these emotions, and that anybody going through similar challenges would have very similar feelings.

In age-appropriate language and without delving into unnecessary details, be frank about past troubles and obstacles ahead, and acknowledge that life will undoubtedly change. Most of all, reassure your child that he or she is loved, wanted, and worthy of all the wonderful gifts that life has to offer.